For Mark, James, Joseph, and Jessica
—J. H.

To Ji-chan and Moley, with love
—M. M.

Atheneum Books for Young Readers
An imprint of Simon & Schuster Children's Publishing Division
1230 Avenue of the Americas, New York, New York 10020
Text copyright © 2006 by Julia Hubery
Illustrations copyright © 2006 by Mei Matsuoka
First published in Great Britain in 2006 by Simon & Schuster UK Ltd, a CBS Company, as *Raffi's Surprise*.

The illustrations for this book are rendered in mixed media.
Manufactured in China
First U.S. edition 2007
2 4 6 8 10 9 7 5 3 1
Library of Congress Cataloging-in-Publication Data
Hubery, Julia.
[Raffi's surprise]
A friend for all seasons / Julia Hubery ; illustrated by Mei Matsuoka.
p. cm.
Originally published: England : Simon & Schuster Childrens Books, 2006, under the title Raffi's surprise.
Summary: Robbie the Raccoon and his friends love Father Oak and worry that he is sick when his leaves begin to turn color and fall off,
but Robbie's mother explains what the change means and helps him plant some acorns as a sign of hope for spring.
ISBN-13: 978-1-4169-2685-6
ISBN-10: 1-4169-2685-2
[1. Seasons—Fiction. 2. Raccoons—Fiction. 3. Forest animals—Fiction. 4. Oak—Fiction. 5. Trees—Fiction.]   I. Matsuoka, Mei, ill.
II. Title.
PZ7.H863166Fri 2007
[E]—dc22
2006025725

A Friend for All Seasons

Julia Hubery

Mei Matsuoka

Atheneum Books for Young Readers

NEW YORK   LONDON   TORONTO   SYDNEY

Robbie Raccoon loved his home.
He loved the long swishy grass, the sparkling
stream, and the rustling trees.
But most of all, Robbie loved . . .

. . . Old Father Oak.

Robbie was born in a cozy den
high in Father Oak's sturdy trunk.
In the spring, he learned to climb
on Father Oak's strong branches.

And all summer long he played with his friends Chip and Blackbird in the shade of Father Oak's green leaves.

On the first day of fall, Robbie woke early, kissed his mother, and tiptoed out to find Chip.

But all Robbie found
was a chilly, silvery mist.

He crept to the end of a branch.
There he found a pretty golden leaf.
Should I pick it? Would Father Oak mind?

Suddenly the leaf dropped, twirling away in the mist.

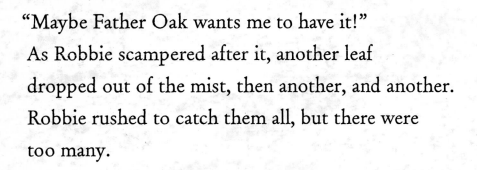

"Maybe Father Oak wants me to have it!"
As Robbie scampered after it, another leaf
dropped out of the mist, then another, and another.
Robbie rushed to catch them all, but there were
too many.

The chilly mist made Robbie shiver.
Maybe Father Oak is cold too, he thought.
So he gathered the leaves and piled them
over Father Oak's roots.
Just then Chip peeked around Father Oak's trunk.

"Robbie, what are you doing?"
"I'm making a blanket for Father Oak. He's losing his leaves because he's cold," answered Robbie.
"But they're still falling," said Chip. "Maybe he's crying."
"Father Oak must be sad. Let's give him a hug!" said Robbie.

The friends put their arms around Father Oak
and hugged him. But still the leaves fell.
"Blackbird, come and help us!" called Robbie.
"Father Oak is crying, so let's hug our hugest hug
and sing our happiest song!"

Their singing woke Robbie's mother.
"What's happening?" she asked.
"Father Oak's crying all his leaves away and
we're trying to cheer him up!" they said.
"Don't worry, little ones. He isn't crying."

"He's telling us that fall is here and winter is coming," Robbie's mother said.

"What is winter?" they asked.

"Winter is a cold, dark, sleepy time when all the leaves and flowers hide and sleep."

"Winter sounds horrible!" said Robbie.

"But without winter, we couldn't get ready for spring," said his mother.

"What should we do with Father Oak's
leaves then?" asked Robbie.
"We'll make our own blankets. It's almost time
for us to take our winter nap," said his mother.
Soon, Robbie saw that all the animals were
busy gathering leaves and food for the winter.

Through the golden fall days, Robbie and his mother
ate and ate, until they were as fat as could be.
"Is it time for our winter nap yet?" Robbie asked.

"Not quite," said his mother. "We still have a favor to
do for Father Oak."
She gave Robbie five acorns.

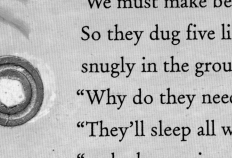

"We must make beds for them," she said.
So they dug five little holes and tucked the acorns
snugly in the ground.
"Why do they need beds?" asked Robbie.
"They'll sleep all winter, just like us," she said,
"and when spring comes . . . well, it's a surprise."

Then they curled up together in their den.
Robbie's mother sang a winter lullaby
until Robbie fell sound asleep.

Snug inside Father Oak, they
drowsed away dark days of wind . . .

and ice . . .

and snow.

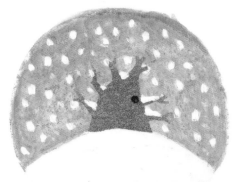

One morning, Robbie woke to a tingle in the air.
He poked his nose out of the den.
Father Oak's branches sparkled with tiny new leaves.
"Mommy!" he shouted. "I think it's spring now!"
She rubbed her eyes and peeked out.

"Look!" cried Robbie excitedly.

There, on the ground below, was a wonderful surprise.
From each little acorn bed, two tiny oak leaves pushed
up into the sun.

"Our acorns have turned into baby oaks!"

"So they have." His mother smiled.
"And if you help Father Oak look after them,
one day they will become big oak trees—
more friends for you to love!"